FAITHFULNESS UNDER FIRE
THE STORY OF GUIDO DE BRES

BY WILLIAM BOEKESTEIN | ILLUSTRATED BY EVAN HUGHES

RHB | REFORMATION HERITAGE BOOKS
Grand Rapids, Michigan

Reformation Heritage Books
2965 Leonard Street, NE,
Grand Rapids, MI 49525
616-977-0889 / Fax 616-285-3246
orders@heritagebooks.org
www.heritagebooks.org

Library of Congress Cataloging-in-Publication Data

Boekestein, William.
Faithfulness under fire : the story of Guido de Brès / by William Boekestein ; illustrated by Evan Hughes.
p. cm.
ISBN 978-1-60178-102-4
1. Brès, Guy de, 1522-1567--Juvenile literature. 2. Reformed Church--Belgium--Clergy--Biography--Juvenile literature. I. Hughes, Evan. II. Title.
BX9480.B6B7428 2010
284'.2092--dc22
[B]
2010031918

For additional Reformed literature, both new and used, request a free book list from Reformation Heritage Books at the above regular or e-mail address.

Printed in the United States of America
12 13 14 15 16 17/11 10 9 8 7 6 5 4 3 2

WANTED

Guido de Bres

Suspect is tall, pale, rather thin with a long face and a reddish beard. He looks disheveled in his black coat.

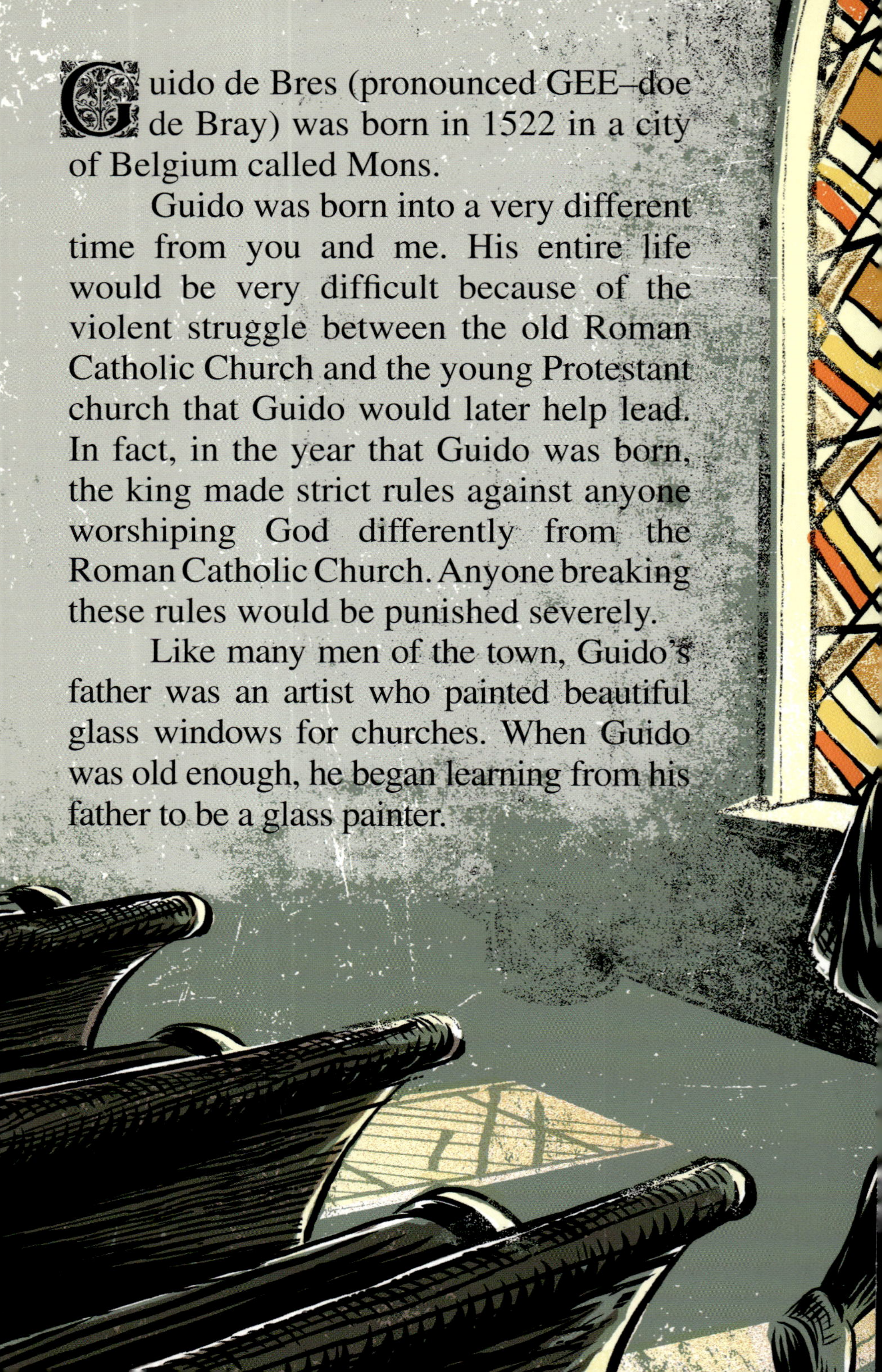

Guido de Bres (pronounced GEE–doe de Bray) was born in 1522 in a city of Belgium called Mons.

Guido was born into a very different time from you and me. His entire life would be very difficult because of the violent struggle between the old Roman Catholic Church and the young Protestant church that Guido would later help lead. In fact, in the year that Guido was born, the king made strict rules against anyone worshiping God differently from the Roman Catholic Church. Anyone breaking these rules would be punished severely.

Like many men of the town, Guido's father was an artist who painted beautiful glass windows for churches. When Guido was old enough, he began learning from his father to be a glass painter.

When Guido was a young man he was given a Bible, which he read with joy. He also read the writings of the Reformers, men like Martin Luther and John Calvin, who loved the church enough to point out some of its problems. This is why the church of the Reformers was called Protestant—it was "protesting" against certain ideas and practices in the Roman Catholic Church.

As Guido studied, God filled the young man's heart with love for Him. After his conversion, Guido felt called to become a minister. As a young man, he left for England, where he had many godly teachers.

Years earlier, when Guido's mother was pregnant with him, she had prayed that her son would become a minister. Her prayer was being answered!

England
N
Edward VI

Back in Guido's hometown of Mons, Reformed Christians were being persecuted. But in England, Guido was able to study peaceably because the king, Edward VI, agreed with the teachings of the Reformers. In fact, many Christians fled to England when Edward was king to escape persecution in their own countries.

Before long, King Edward died, and the new queen of England persecuted Protestants. England was no longer safe for people like Guido. He decided to return to his home country of Belgium, where he became a traveling preacher. Even here his life was constantly in danger. He had to preach in people's homes instead of in a church. He could not use his real name for fear that he would be killed by the enemies of his church.

Guido was not only preaching, he was also writing. His first book was called "The Staff of the Faith." In this book he pointed out some of the problems in the Roman Catholic Church.

This same year, Philip II became ruler of a powerful kingdom called the Holy Roman Empire. Philip was not pleased with the teachings of Guido and his friends. He imprisoned, tortured, or killed many Protestants. A family from Guido's own church was arrested and burned alive. Guido was forced to flee to Switzerland, where he would be safer.

Compared to his difficult life in Belgium, the next several years were good for Guido. He was again able to study the Bible, this time in Geneva, a city in Switzerland. Here he learned from the preaching of John Calvin and the teaching of Theodore Beza, both Protestants. Guido became an expert in Hebrew and Greek, the languages the Bible was written in. He also learned to show mercy to people who were hurting.

After his time of study, Guido was given a great help. He got married! Catherine Ramon married Guido even though she knew that her new life with him would likely be sad and dangerous. Guido and Catherine were blessed with several children. He called her his "dear and beloved wife and sister in our Savior Jesus Christ." Sadly, their life together would last only eight years.

Guido and Catherine settled in a Belgian town called Doornik, where he had to be a pastor in secret. He also began, in secret, to write a paper that explained just what he and his friends believed. This Confession of Faith would become his most well-known and useful piece of work.

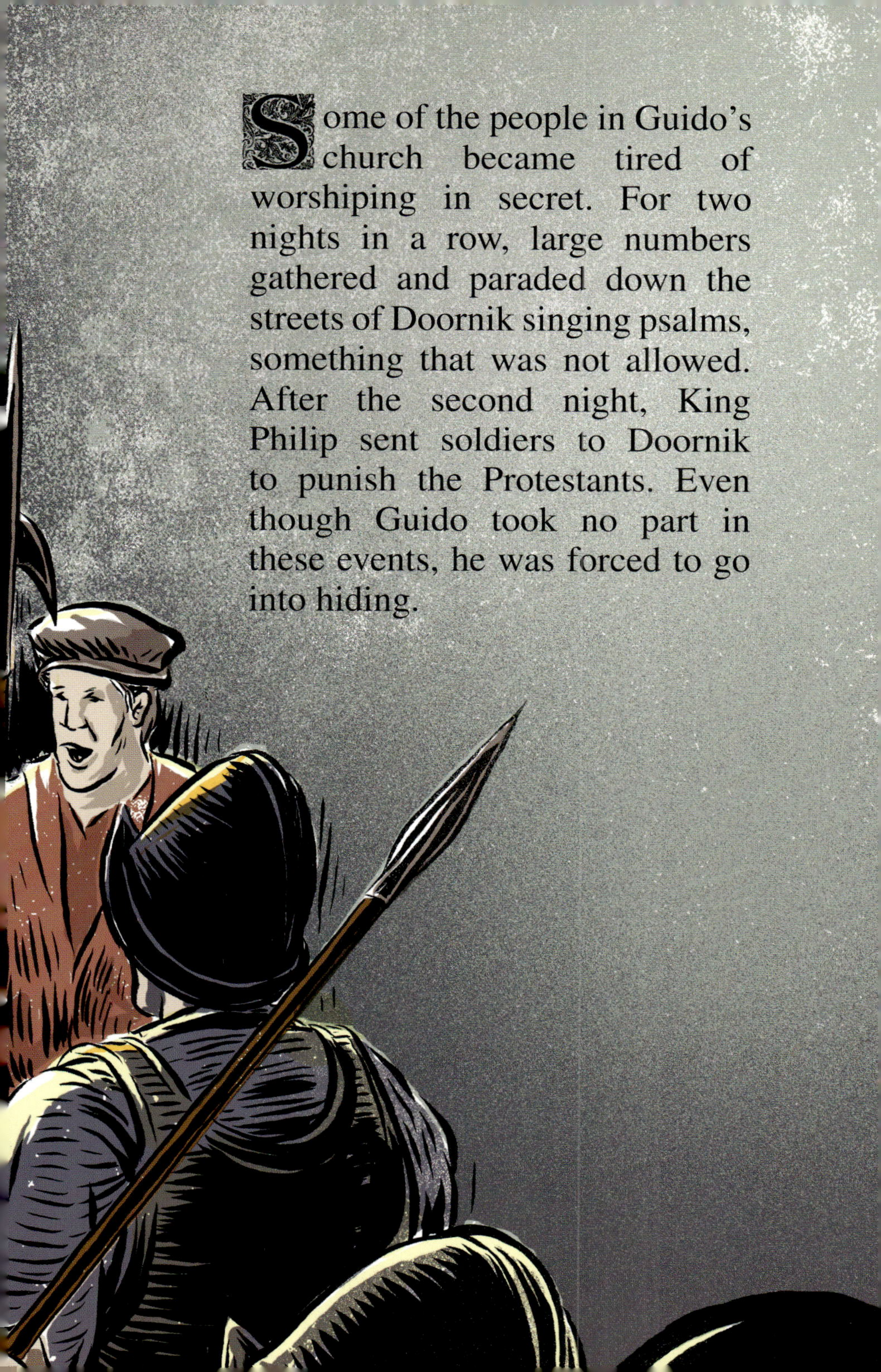

Some of the people in Guido's church became tired of worshiping in secret. For two nights in a row, large numbers gathered and paraded down the streets of Doornik singing psalms, something that was not allowed. After the second night, King Philip sent soldiers to Doornik to punish the Protestants. Even though Guido took no part in these events, he was forced to go into hiding.

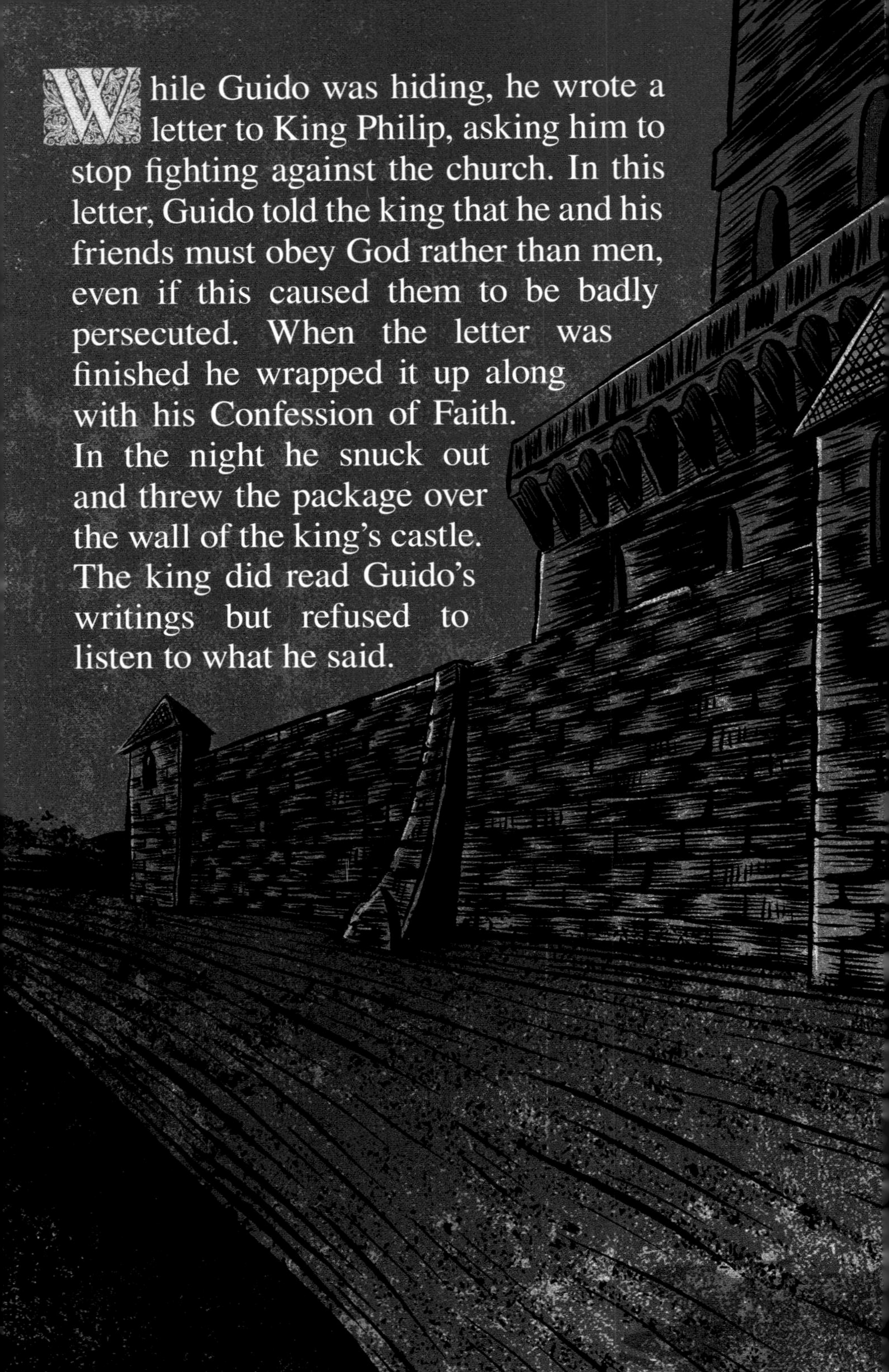

While Guido was hiding, he wrote a letter to King Philip, asking him to stop fighting against the church. In this letter, Guido told the king that he and his friends must obey God rather than men, even if this caused them to be badly persecuted. When the letter was finished he wrapped it up along with his Confession of Faith. In the night he snuck out and threw the package over the wall of the king's castle. The king did read Guido's writings but refused to listen to what he said.

Instead, Guido became hunted more fiercely than before. Again he was forced to flee for his life. When the leaders of the city found out that Guido was gone, they were very angry. They made a life-size figure of Guido and burned it along with all of his belongings that they found in his house.

Although Guido's life was constantly in danger, God was using his work. Guido was able to minister to countless people through his secret preaching and writing.

Many people thought Guido's Confession of Faith was a clear and faithful summary of the Bible. In fact, all of the Reformed churches in Guido's country of Belgium agreed that this would be their official summary of faith. To this day, Guido's confession is called the Belgic Confession.

When Guido was forty-four years old he began to minister in a town called Valenciennes. So many people hungered for his plain Bible teaching that no building could hold the crowds that came. So he began to preach in fields, sometimes to as many as twenty-five thousand people! The men stood on the outside of the crowd armed with pitchforks and other weapons to protect the women and children in the center.

As Protestant Christians began to be more open about their faith, some people went too far. The people had come to believe that the way the Roman Catholic Church worshiped with its images of the saints, its crucifixes, and fancy priestly robes was not the Bible's way. Against Guido's instructions they began to destroy some of the property of the Roman Catholic Church.

When King Philip heard of the Protestant violence, for three months he surrounded the city in which Guido was living. He managed to escape. But the next day someone told Philip's men where Guido was hiding. On an early spring day, Guido was captured and placed in chains.

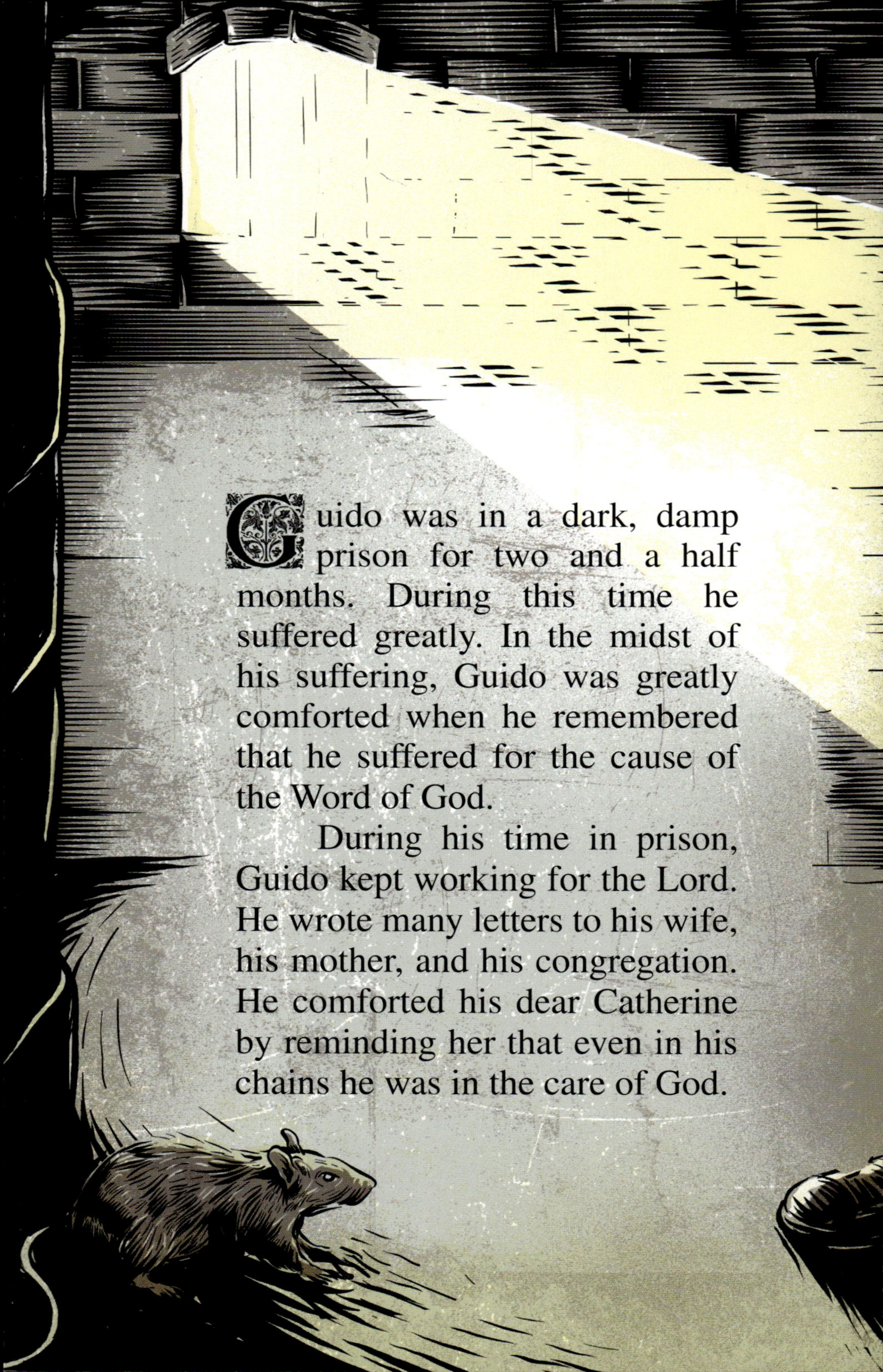

Guido was in a dark, damp prison for two and a half months. During this time he suffered greatly. In the midst of his suffering, Guido was greatly comforted when he remembered that he suffered for the cause of the Word of God.

During his time in prison, Guido kept working for the Lord. He wrote many letters to his wife, his mother, and his congregation. He comforted his dear Catherine by reminding her that even in his chains he was in the care of God.

On the last day of May 1567, the guards came early and woke up Guido and one of his friends, Peregrin. They were to be hanged in front of the town hall. As Guido left the prison he encouraged his fellow prisoners: “I would never have thought that God would have given me such an honor” as to die for Him.

Guido was forced to climb a ladder with a rope around his neck. While he climbed he spoke about God to the people watching below. He also charged them to show proper honor to the men who were putting him to death.

While he was still speaking the guards pushed Guido off the ladder. A few minutes later Guido was dead. His body was disposed of in a shameful manner, but his soul entered into the comfort of his Lord.

By God’s grace, Guido had lived a life in total service to God. And although his life was short and painful, it was not in vain. Through his preaching and writing Guido has helped thousands of people to love and serve God, down to this very day.

The life of Guido de Bres is not exactly a pleasant read. The story is sad, and, in our age of tolerance, at times it is uncomfortable. Yet we believe his story is important because it really happened. In fact, it happened a lot! In other words, de Bres was not all that extraordinary. He was one of countless Christians who spent their lives in devotion to the Lord and in commitment to His Word.

We should say a few things about the graphic details and references to historical religious conflict in this book. First, the reader should know that every reasonable attempt has been made to avoid gratuitous, unsavory detail. It would be impossible, however, to tell the story of de Bres apart from the theme of suffering. We have also tried carefully to avoid unnecessarily inflammatory religious rhetoric. However, the fact remains that right up to the present, strongly held convictions will produce conflict. Even young children experience this.

Second, we don't believe it is necessary to shield even young children from the ugliness of life as long as we also provide a context in which this life can be lived victoriously. Guido de Bres thrived in tragedy because he was hoping in the gospel of Jesus Christ. The gospel (or good news) of Jesus is this: because of His perfect life and sacrificial death, those who repent of their sins and trust in Him have God's promise of forgiveness and eternal life (John 3:16). As this promise is realized in our lives, we too will approach life with the same hope that de Bres had. We will be equipped and motivated to spend our lives for God's glory as we look to an eternal reward of grace.

This is the value we see in teaching our children about Guido de Bres—not to glorify him, but to be drawn by his example to live to the glory of God.

Those interested in further reading on the life and Belgic Confession of Guido de Bres are encouraged to read Thea Van Halsema's *Three Men Came to Heidelberg and Glorious Heretic: The Story of Guido de Bres* (Grand Rapids: I.D.E.A Ministries, 1996). More advanced readers will appreciate Daniel Hyde's *With Heart and Mouth: An Exposition of the Belgic Confession* (Grandville, MI: Reformed Fellowship, 2008). The Belgic Confession is also available at: http://www.puritanseminary.org/media/BelgicConfession.pdf.